RETURN
OF THE
SILVER
CYBORG

ADAM BRITTEN
Illustrated by Arthur Hamer

Piccadilly Press

For Lynn

First published in Great Britain in 2013
by Piccadilly Press,
A Templar/Bonnier publishing company
Deepdene Lodge, Deepdene Avenue,
Dorking, Surrey, RH5 4AT
www.piccadillypress.co.uk

A catalogue record for this book is available
from the British Library

ISBN: 978 1 84812 320 5 (paperback)

1 3 5 7 9 10 8 6 4 2

Printed in the UK by CPI Group (UK) Ltd, Croydon, CR0 4YY
Cover design by Simon Davis
Cover and interior illustrations by Arthur Hamer

SOME STUFF YOU MIGHT NEED TO KNOW

OK, before we get started, let's talk about me. After all, I'm the one telling the story.

My name is Mark Taylor and I'm an Astral Guardian. So are my dad, mum and sister. We've been sent to Earth to protect the world from super villains, aliens and all sorts of nasty stuff. We're part of an intergalactic police force whose job it is to make sure the universe stays safe. Astral Command (who are in charge of just about everything) give us our orders but, if things go wrong, they send the Astral Knights to sort things out.

You don't want to mess with the Astral Knights. They can blow up planets!

Here on Earth we're known as superheroes. Dad is Captain Valiant. He can fly and has super-strength. He also likes bacon sandwiches and eats lots of them, but that's not really a superpower.

Mum is
Ms Victory. She is
super-clever,
super-fast and tells
Dad off for eating
lots of bacon
sandwiches. She does
all the scientific and
technical stuff.

My sister, Emma,
is Moon Girl.
She can move
objects with her
mind and has a cloak of
invisibility. She is also
very moody and
likes to thump me.

I'm Dynamic Boy. Yes, I know it's a stupid name. But if you think that's stupid, you should see my costume. Dad and Mum look great in red, white and blue. Emma is in black and silver, but looks even better when she's invisible. My costume is black and gold with a lightning  flash down the front. I look like an electric bee. Even my powers aren't much good. All I can do is fly and create illusions. Who cares about that?

When they're not being superheroes, Dad and Mum are Robert and Louise Taylor, IT consultants. When we're not being superheroes, Emma and I are just two normal children . . . apart from the superpowers, of course. But we're only allowed to use our powers when we're fighting super villains, aliens and all that other nasty stuff. When we're out with our friends we can't use them. When we're at home or school, Mum and Dad want us to be like everyone else. Superpowers are banned, even though Emma and I sometimes use them when we think Mum and Dad won't find out!

We live in a normal house . . . well, almost normal. We have a laboratory hidden under the washing machine in the utility room. That's where we watch out for all those super villains and aliens. I suppose you could call it our secret base, although it's not very big. It's full of computers and strange machines that I don't understand. It's also the place where we go to contact Astral Command – but we only do that in emergencies. We're meant to be able to do this job on our own.

The only thing in the lab that really impresses

me is the particle web. It can transport us all over the world in an instant, which is very impressive for something that looks like a giant, green, glowing bogey. At least, *I* think it does. Mum's the

only one who really knows how the particle web works and she doesn't like me calling it a giant, green, glowing bogey. She says it's too important to make fun of. Well, she *is* super-clever, so I suppose she knows what she's talking about.

And that's it really. Apart from fighting monsters, super villains and protecting the world from alien attacks, we're just a normal family. Of course, we probably have a few more adventures than most normal families and I imagine, if you've read this far, that you're ready for another one.

Well, here it is . . .

CHAPTER 1

It all began when a cash machine got a bit moody.

No, you can't have any money, the text on the screen said. *I've seen your credit card bill. Pay that first and maybe I'll change my mind.*

The man who was waiting for his money was so surprised he took a picture of the screen and posted it on Facebook. I don't know whether he got his cash, but I do know it wasn't long before a queue formed at the machine with lots of people waiting

to be told off for
spending too much.

It happened in
New York so it was no
surprise that, within
hours, a news team had
turned up. It did come
as a shock when a
grinning reporter with a squeaky voice used the
machine and was told, *You can have as much money as
you like – and if you want my advice you'll go and buy a
new outfit. Green isn't your colour. And as for that hair! Did
you look in the mirror before you left home this morning?*

The reporter burst into tears, dropped her
microphone and ran down the street. The cameraman followed her as she dashed through the crowds.

We watched it on television while having
breakfast in the kitchen. Emma pointed at the
screen and said, 'The cash machine's right. Green
isn't her colour.' She munched on her toast. 'And
her bum's too big for that skirt.'

Mum tipped muesli into a bowl.

'It's a practical joke,' she said.

'I wouldn't wear that skirt even as a joke,' Emma replied.

'No, I mean the cash machine. It's some kind of stunt. Have you noticed no one has typed in their PIN? They just insert their card and the text appears. There must be a hidden camera somewhere.'

Dad stared at the top of a Corn Flakes box, narrowed his eyes and gritted his teeth.

'You'd think they could have made it easier to

close a box,' he said, trying for the third time to get the small cardboard lip under the lid. He pushed the cardboard together and the lip sprang up.

Mum sighed, took the box, closed the lid and passed him the milk.

'Don't spill it,' she said.

Dad always poured the milk too quickly and it always splashed everywhere. Today was no different. He ate his Corn Flakes with a white puddle round his bowl.

'Is there anything else on?' Dad pointed his spoon at the television and dropped a soggy Corn Flake on the table. 'I don't really want to watch a woman with a big bum running down the street.'

I reached for the remote but Mum got there first.

'Leave that alone, Mark,' she said. 'The news is important. Besides, I'm sure it's not that difficult for your father to watch a woman with a big bum. In fact, I think he rather enjoys it.'

Dad went red and Emma tutted.

'Men,' she muttered, banging the jam on the table.

It was only eight o'clock in the morning and already Emma seemed to be in a bad mood. I didn't know why. It was half-term and, even though Astral Guardians never really took holidays, it was nice to have a week when we didn't have to worry about school as well as saving the world. I liked it when the four of us could sit in our dressing gowns and eat breakfast together.

Mornings like this were rare. Even when we weren't chasing super villains or fighting aliens, a normal day could be a bit of a rush. Emma usually spent too much time in the bathroom. Dad couldn't find his car keys. I did the homework that was due in that morning and Mum got angry with all of us for not being more organised.

So even though I yawned, stretched and part of me wished I was still in bed, I enjoyed it as we sat there munching our cereal and slurping our orange juice. I even smiled when Dad pushed his bowl away, drummed his fingers on the table and looked round the kitchen.

'I don't suppose there's any chance of a bacon sandwich?' he said.

Mum's head shot up. I thought she was about to tell Dad what he could do with his bacon sandwich. She had that serious look on her face that usually meant she was going to give him a lecture about not eating fatty food. Instead, she grabbed the remote control and turned up the volume on the television.

'. . . a spate of computer faults with no apparent explanation,' the over-tanned newsreader said. 'Online games have crashed and websites have shut down. Car satellite navigation systems have argued with their drivers and, at Flushing Meadows in New York, a mobile phone, which had been left in the washroom of the Lunch Monkey Café, posted photos of everyone using the toilet on the internet.'

Mum stared at the television. 'First a cash machine insults its users,' she said, 'then a mobile phone takes pictures of people going to the toilet. I don't like this kind of coincidence.'

'Well, it did happen at Flushing Meadows,'

Dad said.

Mum wasn't amused. She was about to say something when she was interrupted by a high-pitched wail. It was so loud the cutlery on the table rattled. Mum sat with her mouth open as we all looked at each other in amazement.

'Is that the intruder alarm or the fire alarm?' Dad said. 'I know we test them regularly but they both sound the same to me.'

'It's the intruder alarm!' Mum shouted. 'Someone's in the lab!'

It was a mad scramble to see who got there

first. Chairs scraped, the table clattered and crockery smashed. Not surprisingly, Mum reached the washing machine before anyone else – she was, after all, super-fast – and pressed the controls to open the secret door. Nothing happened.

She was about to try again when Dad told us to stand back, dug his fingers into the washing machine and ripped it out of the floor.

Unfortunately, Dad seemed to have forgotten that the washing machine was plumbed in. As it came away from the wall, water spurted out of broken pipes. The glass door cracked as he dropped the washing machine behind him and leapt into the secret corridor to the laboratory.

Soap suds and wet
clothes swilled around our feet.

Emma screamed and pointed at the
clothes. 'There's a red sock in with my white
blouses!' she said. 'Who put a red sock in with
my white blouses?!'

I didn't know what she was on about.
I couldn't see any white blouses. They all
looked pink to me.

I suppose we should have waited for Dad to find out what was going on before following him. After all, he is Captain Valiant.

If anyone had to get in trouble first, then it should be him. But none of us did wait. With Mum in front, me behind and Emma at the back, we crowded into the corridor and ran into the lab.

Once we were inside, no one seemed to know what to do. The alarm continued to howl. Dad stood at a control panel and looked as if he was trying to remember how to turn it off. Mum pushed past him and typed in the code. Even before the wailing stopped, she turned to face the room.

'This isn't possible,' she said. 'This just isn't possible.'

It might not have been possible but it had happened. Usually, the lab was a riot of colour with flashing red, yellow and green lights. There was always something whirring or bleeping. The lab was our eyes and ears on the world. It never shut down. We couldn't do our job as Astral Guardians if the lab shut down. And yet everything was quiet. We stared at rows and rows of blank screens and monitors. There wasn't a single light flashing. It was as if the room had died.

Mum went from screen to screen and from panel to panel, pushing buttons and flicking switches. Every time her fingers turned something on, she said the same thing: 'This isn't possible.'

Emma had more important things to worry about than Mum's computers. She held up a dripping pink blouse and glared at us.

'Who put a red sock in the washing machine?' she said again.

We all ignored her.

'Louise, are you sure it was the intruder alarm?' Dad said. 'There's no one here. Maybe we should get the tones changed.

It would make it so much easier to know what was going on if we got the tones changed.'

Mum groaned and sat at a keyboard. She stared at it as if she didn't know what the keys were for. Her hand went to type something but her fingers didn't know what to type.

'If someone doesn't tell me who put a red sock in the washing machine,' Emma said, 'there's going to be serious trouble.'

We all ignored her.

'I suppose this means we have a lot to do today,' Dad said, patting his stomach. 'It could take quite a while to fix whatever's gone wrong in here. So, before we start, does anyone fancy a bacon sandwich?'

Mum groaned again and put her head in her hands. 'You know what?' she said. 'That's sounds like a good idea. Why don't you all go upstairs and have a bacon sandwich? I'd like to be alone for a while.'

I couldn't believe it. Mum said we could have bacon sandwiches. That's when I knew that whatever had happened, it was a lot more serious than I had thought.

CHAPTER 2

Mum did her best to sort things out, but nothing worked. She spent the rest of the morning on her hands and knees with her head in the back of a computer or behind a wall panel. Every time I went down to ask if I could help, I spoke to her bottom as she unscrewed circuits and pulled at knots of multicoloured wires. It looked as if she knew what she was doing, but every so often she muttered and swore and sat up with a red face.

Dad wasn't much use. He sat at a keyboard pressing whatever keys Mum told him to press. I don't think he minded. After all, he was the one who couldn't close a cereal box.

'You were right, Mum,' I said, trying to make her smile as she reached for a pair of pliers. 'Dad doesn't find it difficult to stare at a woman with a big bum.'

She glared at me. 'Is that supposed to be funny?'

Dad grinned, but quickly realised it wasn't a good idea to grin. I realised it was probably a good idea to go back upstairs. Emma and I had been told to stay in the kitchen and watch the news. At least I couldn't get in trouble if I watched the news.

'Has anything happened?' I asked as I sat at the table. It had been a long time since breakfast and, because Mum and Dad were busy in the lab, we'd done our bit to help by making sure the kitchen was as clean and tidy as Mum liked it.

'The chocolate biscuits are gone,' Emma replied.

'I thought you said I could have the last one.'

Emma shrugged. 'There are too many cookery programmes on TV. I was hungry.'

'But you were supposed to be watching the news.'

Emma mumbled something under her breath, got up and went to a cupboard. She bent down and searched through neat rows of packets and boxes.

'You're so boring,' she said. 'If we watch the

25

news then we might see something that means we have to go out and be superheroes. Can't we have some time off for a change?' She reached to the back of the cupboard, found a packet of custard creams, returned to the table, tore open the wrapper and started to crunch.

'Do you want one?' she asked with her mouth full.

I shook my head. 'No, thanks. I prefer my pasta cooked.'

'Pasta? What are you talking about? These are —'

Emma coughed and spat. The packet of Custard Creams became a packet of dried pasta. Of course, it had always been a packet of dried pasta. When your brother has the power to create illusions, it's best not to annoy him. I had really wanted that last chocolate biscuit.

But, then again, when your sister has the power to move objects with her mind, it's best not to sit on a chair with your back to the sink.

I was lucky – I heard the tap  squeak, and Emma was still coughing on the pasta, which meant her aim was off. Water spurted over my head.

The television wasn't so lucky. It got soaked. There was a loud bang and a flash. The bang was loud enough to bring Mum and Dad running up from the lab.

We didn't need to explain what had happened. Mum and Dad knew us too well. I expected one of them to shout, but they both looked as if they had other things on their minds.

'I'm sorry,' I said. 'I was only —'

'It was his fault,' Emma said, picking bits of pasta from her teeth. 'I almost choked. Look at that!' She opened her mouth and pointed at her tongue. 'Itsth really thore.'

'Then why don't you be quiet and let the rest of us do the talking,' a voice said.

Emma's finger hovered over her mouth. Slowly, she turned to look at the television. The screen was blank and there was smoke coming

from the sides, but there was no doubt about it – the television had told her to be quiet.

'That's better,' the television said. 'I hope I have your attention now.'

As if it was the most normal thing in the world to hear a television speak, Mum sat at the table and waited. Dad raised his fist and looked as if he was about to attack the set. Mum shook her head and pointed to the chair next to her. Dad did as he was instructed. Mum coughed to clear her throat.

'I've been expecting you,' she said. 'I wasn't quite sure how you'd make contact. You've made quite a mess of my communication systems. But cash machines and mobile phones weren't going to hold your interest for long. So how are you, Algernon? It's been a while since we last met.'

The television laughed. 'I'm very well, thank you, Ms Victory. And you're right, the cash machines and the mobile phones weren't going to hold my interest for long. On the other hand, air traffic control systems and railway networks will be much more fun. Just think what I could do to them. But before

this gets nasty, tell me, when did you work out I was responsible for your systems failure?'

'It took some time,' Mum replied. 'I had to restore the power first. Once that was done, the system scan did the rest. The virus you uploaded was very distinctive, and I knew there was only one man who could get through my firewalls.'

The television sparked.

'Of course there was only one man who could outwit you, Ms Victory. I'm Algernon Pratt: the Silver Cyborg. I'm the greatest computer genius who ever lived. Your security systems were never going to stop me, just as you must have known that a prison was never going to hold me. A man with my talents is far too valuable to the government. You shouldn't put your faith in the law, Ms Victory. I'd done a deal within weeks of my capture.'

Dad pointed at the television. 'Let me smash it,' he said. 'That'll shut him up.'

'Yes, go on, smash the television,' Pratt replied. 'Your stupid daughter almost ruined everything with her pathetic tantrum, so why don't you finish the job? I had everything planned: the news reports about machines going wrong, your systems failure, the intruder alarm going off so that you would find out what I'd done and then, when I was ready, I was going to transmit a special broadcast to this television explaining my demands. Now, I might as

well have sent a text message. Do you know how long it's taken me to track you down, access your database and find out all your secrets?'

'Well, it's been about a year since you went to prison,' Dad said.

'That's right, about a —' Pratt fell silent. 'Well, since I have no choice now, I suppose I'd better make this quick. This television could pack up at any moment. Captain Valiant, you and your team have thirty minutes to reach Stonehenge. Don't ask why and don't get anyone else involved. Just make sure the four of you are at Stonehenge in half an hour. Otherwise I start playing games with planes, trains and anything else that amuses me.

'And no tricks. Make sure Dynamo Boy doesn't try any illusions. I want the four of you at Stonehenge in person. And just to make sure you do as I say, let me show you one of the new toys I've developed. It's called a sonic bomb. I want you to imagine what would happen if this started going off in people's homes.'

The Cyborg laughed. The laugh got louder and

louder until
the television
started to
vibrate and
rattle. Then it
exploded. We
all ducked as
plastic and
glass shot

over our heads, smashed against the
wall and thudded into the

cupboards. A tangle
of green and brown
wires flew from the back of the
set. The bare ends twisted and
jerked as sparks bounced across

the wet floor before going out with a sizzle.

Emma coughed and wiped her
eyes. Dad stared at the television
as if expecting it to do something
else. Mum gritted her teeth and
glared at the smouldering plastic.

'Algernon Pratt,' she said. 'The first super villain we fought when we arrived on Earth. He almost took control of the world's banking systems. How could anyone have been stupid enough to let him near a computer again?'

'Because he's a genius,' Dad replied. 'Think what he could do for the government. There isn't a computer he couldn't hack or a secret he couldn't find out.'

'I know,' Mum said. 'It's our computer he's hacked and our secrets he's found out.'

Dad frowned and thumped the table, only he thumped it too hard. The legs at his end snapped and sent what was left of the television flying across the room. The set smashed through the kitchen window, went over the garden fence and splashed into our neighbour's ornamental pond.

'Before we get changed and do the superhero thing,' Emma said, 'it might be a good idea if someone went next door and explained to Mr Jones why there's a television swimming around with his koi carp.'

CHAPTER 3

Dynamo Boy! The Silver Cyborg called me *Dynamo Boy*! Why was my name so hard to remember? If it wasn't bad enough having our computers attacked and our television blown up, the Silver Cyborg couldn't even get my name right!

I didn't sulk as I got changed into my costume, but I wasn't in a good mood either. Usually, I tried not to get annoyed when things like this happened.

But it's hard when, no matter how super you are, people forget your name. It's all about powers, you see. I know I should have been used to it by now. I know that being able to create illusions should be just as important as super-strength, super-speed or being able to move objects with your mind. But sometimes I felt I'd be a lot more popular if I'd gone on a TV talent show.

If I performed illusions in a ridiculous costume on television, then everyone would remember my name. I'd be in the papers and everything. Instead, I'm the superhero that everyone forgets. I'm Thingy Boy or You-Know-The-One-In-The-Silly-Costume Boy or What's-He-Called-Again Boy. And, even if they do remember my name, they spell Dynamic wrong!

'I've managed to get the essential systems back online,' Mum said as we gathered in the lab, 'and I've run a safety check on the particle web. Automatic coordinate control is working so there's no chance of us popping out on top of someone. I've also recalibrated the retrieval signal so we should be able to access the web when we need to come home.'

She drummed her fingers on a desk as the screen in front of her showed columns of numbers and symbols. I noticed a flash drive in the console next to the screen. Mum waited for a few moments then removed the flash drive and slipped it into her costume.

'But I'm not going to lie to you.' She turned to look at us. 'This is going to be tough. I'm sure you remember how lucky we were the last time we fought the Silver Cyborg. I doubt he'll make the same mistake again.'

Lucky? I wouldn't have called it luck. I would have called it a miracle!

In the early days, when we first arrived on Earth, we not only had to get used to working as a team but we also had to acclimatise ourselves to the planet. Back on our own world, the weather is strictly controlled. You know when it's going to be sunny and when it's going to rain. All the main centres of population are built under huge domes that protect people from our sun's radiation. On Earth, people move about freely and nature controls the weather rather than an environmental management system.

And that's why
Mum said we were
lucky. The day we
caught the Silver
Cyborg, Dad had a bad cold. Unlike the rest of us,
he found it hard to get used to the changes in the
weather and he was often ill. It would have been
easy enough for Mum to cure him using the
machines in the lab, but she said his body had to
learn to fight off viruses by itself. Dad said it didn't
look good if Captain Valiant turned up to a fight
with a runny nose and a cough.

Thankfully, Mum won the argument – because
if Dad hadn't been suffering with a cold that day,
the Silver Cyborg would have beaten us.

Once we were inside the Cyborg's secret base
and had fought our way through his defences –
nothing spectacular,
just the usual kind of
thing: machine guns,
lasers and flame
throwers – we found

Pratt in his main operations suite. Realising he was finished, Pratt tried to operate an emergency program that would have deleted all his data and made it virtually impossible to prove he had been trying to take over the world's banks. The switch for this program was operated by thumbprint.

Now, just as Pratt went to put his thumb on the touchpad, Dad sneezed and a huge ball of snot flew from his nose and splattered on the pad. When the Cyborg's thumb hit the pad, nothing happened. Instead of activating the program, all Pratt got was a thumb covered in snot. Dad's cold had given us time to drag the Cyborg away from his computers and save the data.

But Mum was right, we wouldn't get that lucky again. We couldn't rely on Dad's snotty nose to save the day!

The particle web did its job without any problem. When we stepped out on the other side, it was a typical, dreary summer's afternoon. The sky was grey and there was a fine mist of rain. Given the fact that Stonehenge is one of the most famous

stone circles in the world, the weather hadn't put off the tourists. There were lots of red, green and blue cagoules gathered in hushed groups. Stonehenge was that kind of place – it made you want to be quiet, which was weird when you remembered that the Ministry of Defence used Salisbury Plain for military exercises.

The only excitement today, though, was the sight of three brightly coloured superheroes walking out of a glowing, green ball. Emma was with us, but she always wore the cloak of invisibility when there was a chance she might be seen close-up by a member of the public. The rest of us had to wear masks, but Emma had a choice: either wear a mask or don't be seen. Since she scowled, frowned or glowered most of the time, it was probably better that she wasn't seen!

Our sudden appearance caused a small ripple in the crowd. Cameras and mobile phones changed

direction and flashed at us.

'Don't worry, everybody,' Dad said in his best commanding tone. 'There's nothing to be concerned about. Everything's completely fine.'

'No, it isn't,' Emma muttered, 'otherwise we wouldn't be here.'

'Just keep calm and carry on,' Dad continued. 'I promise, there's absolutely nothing wrong.'

I understood what Dad was doing. He didn't want to frighten anyone and cause a panic. But in my experience, if you want to convince people there's nothing wrong, you should never tell them there's nothing wrong. They won't believe you. So I wasn't surprised when the hushed groups started to raise their voices and anxious parents called for their children. Rushing feet splashed through wet grass as people hurried back to cars and coaches. Doors slammed, engines fired into life, gears crunched and, in a few minutes, Stonehenge was deserted.

Or it would have been deserted if not for the man in a green jacket who stood in the middle of the stone circle watching us. He waved.

'Hello?' he shouted. 'I'm over here. I'm so glad you made it on time.'

It was Algernon Pratt, the Silver Cyborg, looking like just another tourist on a wet afternoon. As we approached, it was obvious he hadn't changed much since we'd last met. He was still tall and thin, with unruly grey hair that seemed to grow in tufts. His nose stuck out of his face as if it had been glued on and his eyes were set so far back in his head that they were permanently darkened by his bony brows. You could tell he was a man who didn't spend much time in the open air. The only exercise Algernon Pratt took was the kind that worked his mind.

'Where's Moon Girl?' Pratt demanded as we entered the stone circle.

Emma took off her hood so she could be seen.

'Good,' Pratt said, rubbing his skeletal hands together. 'The four of you are here, just as I asked. Now, if you'd like to come this way.'

He took what looked like a remote control out

of his pocket and
pressed a yellow
button.

Nothing happened.

He pressed the
button again.

Still nothing
happened.

He pointed the
remote control at one
of the standing stones
and pressed it a third
time. He went close to
the stone, moved away
from the stone, raised
the remote and
lowered the remote.

Still nothing
happened.

'Ah,' he said. 'Sorry
about this.
I should have checked.'

He searched in his pockets and brought out a pack of batteries. He flicked open the back of the remote control. 'It's always annoying when this happens, isn't it?' He changed the batteries. 'It should work now.'

He pressed the yellow button again. This time, a square hole opened up near the base of one of the stones to reveal a narrow flight of steps.

'If you'll follow me,' he said. 'And do be careful, it's a bit steep.'

Pratt went down the first few steps, stopped and turned back. None of us had moved. He laughed and scratched his head.

'All right then, stay here if you want,' he said, grinning. 'But if you do, and this door closes behind me, you'll never know what I'm planning to do and you'll never be able to stop me.'

'On the other hand,' Dad replied, 'we could capture you now, let the police know where your secret base is and take it easy for the rest of the day.'

Pratt shrugged and disappeared underground. His voice echoed out of the hole. 'You might do that,' he called, 'but I never said this was *my* secret base. However, I will admit there's a lot down here that you'll find interesting.' His head appeared again. 'Now, as I said, watch your step. I don't want any of you to come to any harm . . . At least, not yet.'

49

CHAPTER 4

Why was it that everyone who had a secret base always seemed to have one that was better than ours? We had a laboratory hidden under a washing machine. It was a small, cramped room with lots of computers. Everyone else had huge complexes underground, or in the air, or under the sea. Maybe there was a special company that you could hire to build a secret base – a kind of *Secret-Bases-R-Us*.

Pratt was very pleased with this new base. He glowed with pride as we reached the bottom of the steps and he led us into a large, circular room with a domed ceiling. Of course, the glow may have been sweat. The room was a long way down and, while the four of us managed the descent without any problem, Pratt was out of breath.

I watched him wipe his brow with a handkerchief. The lights set into the wall above our heads turned his face pink.

Maybe if there'd been a lift, he wouldn't have looked so pink. I mean, if you're going to build a secret base underground then you really should have a lift. Pratt was the kind of man who looked like he needed a lift.

'Here we are then.' Pratt wiped his brow again. This time he also wiped his lips. His voice was dry and cracked, as if he needed a drink. 'It doesn't look much, but don't let that fool you. What you see here is the greatest invention in the history of computing. It is more than a machine. It is the next step in human evolution!'

He paused, as if expecting us to gasp or clap or do something to show we were impressed.

We didn't.

'All right, so you probably think I'm exaggerating,' he said. 'But trust me, you've never seen anything like this before.'

Well, that was true. It was one of the strangest

53

rooms I'd ever seen. There was nothing in it. The walls were lined with black and white panels that seemed to be made of metal. The panels went up into the roof and were topped by a small grey disc. The floor was covered in black and white tiles that felt spongy underfoot.

'I don't think much of the colour scheme,' Emma said.

'Genius doesn't have to look good,' Pratt replied. 'What goes on here merely has to work.'

'But still,' Emma said, 'a bit of colour and a few ornaments could really make this a nice place.'

Pratt said something under his breath and walked across to the wall. He laid his hand on a black panel. Strands of light flickered around his fingers.

'I didn't build this place to be nice. I built it to prove, once and for all, that I am the greatest intellect the world has ever known. This is my crowning achievement. I have brought you here so that you may experience my genius firsthand and so that you may know the true power of the Silver Cyborg.'

Dad clenched his fists and strode towards Pratt. 'I'll show you power,' he said. 'The problem with men like you is that you expect everyone to be impressed by big ideas. Well, I'll show you what happens to big ideas.' Dad looked round. 'I don't care what you've built or what you're planning to do with it. All I know is that if I do enough damage, you're finished.'

Pratt folded his arms and leant against the wall.

'You know, if there's one thing I admire about you, Captain Valiant, it's the complete confidence you have in your own stupidity. Go ahead, throw a few punches, knock a few holes in the wall. It won't make any difference.'

'It will when we put you back in prison,' Dad said.

Pratt laughed. He laughed so hard he started to cough.

'Oh that's priceless,' he chortled. 'You haven't worked it out yet, have you? You really are as idiotic as you look. Ms Victory, please, tell the brave and fearless Captain Valiant why you won't be putting me back in prison.'

We all looked at Mum.

She shrugged. 'I think this is the deal he made with the government,' she said. 'That's what he meant when he said this wasn't *his* secret base. It's *their* secret base. The Ministry of Defence owns most of the land round here. I think the government released him from prison so that he could build whatever this is.'

'Well done, Ms Victory,' Pratt said, 'but I'm a little disappointed if that's all you've worked out. I think Lightning Boy could have guessed that much.'

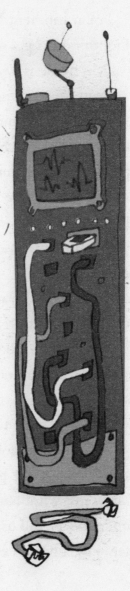

For a moment I wondered who he meant by Lightning Boy.

'My name is *Dynamic* Boy,' I said.

Pratt ignored me.

'Surely you must have an idea of what I've achieved here?' he said to Mum. 'No? Then perhaps a small demonstration might help. It's not much, just a little something I prepared earlier.' He took off his coat, straightened his shirt sleeves, pulled up his trousers, looked down at his shoes as if making sure they were clean, and then announced, 'Protocol activation alpha-sigma-delta-four. Initiate.'

Two panels above Pratt's head glittered with silver dots. The dots joined together in lines, then shapes and then became a picture. It was like watching a huge television.

'Satellite technology is wonderful, isn't it?' Pratt said. 'I'm sure the public would be shocked if they knew just what could be seen from all those miles up in space. And as for military satellites, well, they see just about everything.' He pointed at the

panels. 'I take it you recognise where we are?'

We did. It was our next-door neighbour's back garden. It was easy to recognise because we had forgotten to remove our broken television from Mr Jones's ornamental pond. There he was now, on the screen, staring down into the water with a horrified expression.

'I knew there was something we should have done before we left,' Dad said.

'I wouldn't worry about that if I were you,'
Pratt said. 'It won't be long before your
neighbour has much more on his mind than a
broken television.' He grinned. 'Protocol activation
alpha-sigma-delta-four-gamma. Initiate.'

Mr Jones glanced up. It was as if someone had
called his name. He looked over his shoulder,

frowned and then looked down at the pond again. The next moment, he jumped into the water and began grabbing the fish that swam round his legs.

He picked them up and threw them on the bank. One by one, Mr Jones's very expensive koi carp ended up on the grass, wriggling and writhing. He did nothing to help them.

He carried on catching more fish until there were none left and he stood, staring down at the water. Only then did he seem to notice the fish on the bank. By this time, most of them were dead.

'Protocol termination alpha-sigma-delta-four,' Pratt said.

The image dissolved into silver dots again. Before we lost sight of Mr Jones, we saw him shake his head and stare at his fish. His mouth opened in what looked like a cry and then the image was gone.

'You see, machines are too easy to control,' Pratt said, putting his hands behind his back and striding across the floor, as if giving a lecture. 'You saw that for yourself this morning. Cash machines, mobile phones, even your own computer system; they're no longer a challenge for me. They don't think or react. They merely follow instructions. But the human mind . . . now that's different. What if someone could invent a way of controlling the human mind? That would change the world in ways we can't begin to imagine . . . or should I say, *couldn't* begin to imagine. The fact is, I *have* invented a way of controlling the human mind.' He raised his arms and looked up into the dome. 'And this is it!'

He closed his eyes and sighed.

'But I'm being too modest. I'm not telling you the whole truth. There is so much more.' He looked at us again. 'The true mark of my genius is not the machine. It is the man.'

He put his hand on his forehead and dug his nails into the skin. With two sharp tugs he pulled the skin off his face to reveal a glistening, silver skull. He tapped the metal with his knuckles.

'You see, Ms Victory, this is the actual deal I made with the government. Once I called myself the Silver Cyborg. Now I *am* the Silver Cyborg. I have built the world's most powerful mind – and you're standing in the middle of it!'

CHAPTER 5

This time, he really did expect us to gasp, clap or do something that showed we were impressed. I had the feeling that if we had done something, even if it had only been to nod in appreciation, he would have taken a bow. The way he stood in front of us grinning, it was as if he could already hear the applause.

'What I don't understand,' Emma said, pointing at Pratt's silver skull, 'is why you went to all the trouble of putting metal in your head but did nothing about your hair. A new hairstyle would have done a lot for your image.'

'My image?' Pratt looked at the four of us in turn. 'I've just taken control of your neighbour's mind, made him kill his fish and all you're bothered about is my image?'

'Well, there are a few other things,' Mum said. 'I mean, it's obvious you're telling the truth about what you've built here. But what I don't understand is *why* you've been so honest. Now that you have a machine that can control people's minds, wouldn't it be better not to tell anyone — especially us? You know we'll have do something about it.'

'And,' Dad said, going up to Pratt and glaring at him, 'don't think we've forgotten about the fish.'

Pratt shook his head. He seemed confused. 'Am I the only one in the room who's been paying attention? You're standing inside the world's most powerful brain. I have the ability to make anyone do what I want and you still think you can threaten me?'

Maybe it was Pratt's smug tone that made Dad raise his fist, or maybe he was really annoyed about Mr Jones's fish. Whatever it was, his arm flew up and was about to come crashing down when there was a

hiss and a

CLUNK

Four panels in the walls slid open and four large grey cylinders pointed at us. I didn't know what they were but they didn't look like the kind of things it was a good idea to ignore. Dad must have thought the same. He didn't hit Pratt, although he didn't lower his fist either.

'Of course,' Pratt said, 'despite my undoubted genius, sometimes the old-fashioned methods are the best. You are looking at four sonic cannons and they're set at a frequency that

will shatter you
like eggs.
Obviously, I've
taken precautions
to protect myself,
but I have to be
honest, I'm not
looking forward to
clearing up the

mess. So, if you don't mind, can we forget the
threats and the violence.' He walked to the centre
of the room. 'Besides, those cannons are nothing
compared to what
I have planned. I
promise you, it
gets much better.'
He paused.
'Protocol
activation alpha-
one. Initiate.'

A chair made
of the same black

and white metal as the walls rose from the floor. It was big and bulky with square arms and a wide, rectangular back. It looked very uncomfortable. As Pratt lowered himself into the seat, there was a click. His body seemed to fit into the chair like a plug in a socket. Once he sat down, a small round hole opened in the back of his metal skull. Pratt rested his head against the chair and there was another click.

'Since you're worried about my image, Moon Girl,' he said, 'you should know that there's more than metal in my head. There's a processor that would be the envy of every computer manufacturer in the world. I am now a technological masterpiece.'

As he spoke, the grey disc in the roof started to glow. Ribbons of energy, like small lightning bolts, flickered over the surface.

'It's incredible, isn't it, Ms Victory,' Pratt said, 'that anyone would trust a man like me with something as powerful as this? But what you have to understand is that, in a world such as ours, every politician wants the power to control people and

events. That's why the government made the mistake of doing a deal with me. But they were fools. Did they really imagine I'd swap one prison for another? I'm not going to work for them for the rest of my life. I want my freedom.'

Pratt closed his eyes again.

'Protocol activation omega–three. Initiate.'

His eyes opened.

'But if I'm being honest, it's not just about freedom. It's also about pride. This is my invention. The government might have given me the money to build it, but it's still my design. If they think I'm going to let them have it, they're very much mistaken. This is only a prototype. It works well enough on individuals, but I'm going to build a far more powerful version, one that will control whole groups of people.'

He chuckled to himself.

'Imagine the crimes I could commit by controlling teams of police and security guards. Sometimes one person isn't enough to do a job properly. You have to choose the right individuals

and make them work together. Do you realise, with my new machine, I could become the richest man on the planet?'

'So that's what this is all about?' Mum said. 'Money?'

Pratt took a deep breath and sighed. He looked as if he was about to cry.

'Tell me, Ms Victory, do you know what it's like to grow up without knowing where your next meal will come from? Do you know what it's like

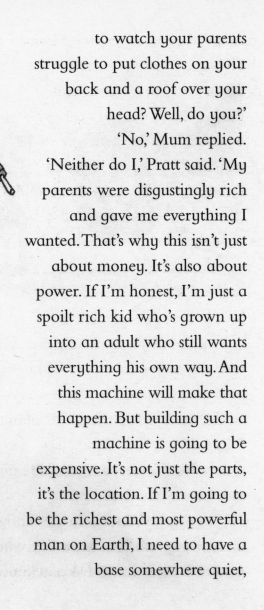

to watch your parents struggle to put clothes on your back and a roof over your head? Well, do you?'

'No,' Mum replied.

'Neither do I,' Pratt said. 'My parents were disgustingly rich and gave me everything I wanted. That's why this isn't just about money. It's also about power. If I'm honest, I'm just a spoilt rich kid who's grown up into an adult who still wants everything his own way. And this machine will make that happen. But building such a machine is going to be expensive. It's not just the parts, it's the location. If I'm going to be the richest and most powerful man on Earth, I need to have a base somewhere quiet, secluded and very private. Maybe I'll buy a couple of islands in the South Pacific. Unfortunately, the last time I tried to steal large amounts of money, you got in the way and I ended up in prison. I'm not going to make that mistake again. Getting the cash will be easy enough, after all I have the power to control people's minds. Making sure you don't interfere is going to be a little more difficult.'

Pratt closed his eyes and his forehead twitched.

'Protocol activation omega-two. Initiate.'

His eyes opened slowly this time. He blinked as if he couldn't see clearly. 'That's why I have ...' His body jerked and he swore under his breath. 'Ouch, that hurt. What on earth ...' Pratt looked up

at the disc. 'There must be some kind of feedback. I suppose it was only to be expected once the program started. The neural net isn't as stable as I'd like. Accessing four minds at the same time was always going to test its capacity. That's why I couldn't risk trying to control you at a distance . . . Maybe I should . . . No, everything's ready now. I can't wait.'

He cleared his throat.

'I have a speech,' he said.

'Do you want to hear it?'

'Not really,' Dad replied. 'I suppose it's the usual kind of thing. You know, the don't-try-to-escape-because-you-can't speech, or the I'm-going-to-have-my-revenge-on-you speech, or the I'm-going-to-take-over-the-world speech – which will probably end with a manic laugh.'

'It's actually a bit of all three,' Pratt said.

'Then can we just have the highlights?'

'Oh, that's a shame, I'd rehearsed it and everything. But still, if that's what you want, I can afford to be generous. After all, you *can't* escape, I *am* going to have my revenge and I *am* going to take over the world, so let's get down to the nitty-gritty, shall we?' He paused. 'Let's talk about Wonder Boy.'

'My name is . . .' I said, but then stopped. 'Actually, I quite like the sound of Wonder Boy.'

Pratt didn't seem to hear me.

'It's very simple really,' he continued. 'I don't plan to kill you or control you the way I did your next-door neighbour. No, that would be too easy. What I want is to make you feel like complete failures. I'm going to create the world's greatest criminal organisation and the people who follow my orders will be the innocent members of the public you try to protect. I will get inside the heads of law-abiding men, women and children and turn them all into thieves and murderers. I want you to live every day knowing that, even with all your

powers, you couldn't save them from me, Algernon Pratt, the Silver Cyborg!' His expression hardened, as if his features had turned to metal. 'Protocol activation omega-one. Initiate!'

There was a sharp crack. Lightning shot from the grey disc down the walls. It snaked across the floor, turning the black and white tiles silver . . . and then everything changed. The room disappeared, Pratt disappeared and the four of us found ourselves back at Stonehenge – only it was a bit different from the Stonehenge we'd last seen. There were no tourists. There was no one in a cagoule. There were lots of people, but they were dressed in animal skins, and most of them were men with knives and spears.

'Illusions,' I heard Pratt's voice say, 'this is all about illusions. I am now in control of Dynamo Boy's mind. His power belongs to me. You're going to fight his illusions while I steal the money I need to build my machine. Once that's done, I'll set you free. Naturally, I'll be gone by then. You can try to find me, but remember, I've had a year to prepare

for this. You'll be wasting your time. However, as soon as my new machine is ready, I'll be in touch.

'For now, just enjoy yourselves. Consider this a preview of what I am going to do if you interfere with my plans ever again; and since this is only a preview, I'll make sure you don't hurt yourselves, but you *will* experience pain. After all, there has to be a bit of reality in a good illusion. But the real pain won't begin until the next time we meet. Then I will hurt you in ways you cannot possibly imagine.'

CHAPTER 6

And that was it. His voice faded and Pratt was gone.

'OK,' Emma said, looking round. 'So this is an illusion, right? It's not real and we've nothing to worry about.'

I wished Emma had been right. The fact was, we had a lot to worry about. This may have been an illusion, but that didn't mean we were safe. The grass, the sky and the stone circle: it all seemed very real to me – and the way the men in animal skins looked around with frightened expressions, they must have heard Pratt's voice as well. They also didn't seem too pleased by our sudden appearance, or that we were dressed in costumes that were a bit different from what they were wearing.

'So this is what's inside your mind,' Emma said to me. 'You really are the most boring person I know. Why couldn't you dream up something with a few more home comforts?'

'I did Stonehenge for a history project,' I replied. 'I got an A.'

'Oh that's brilliant. Not only are we fighting another madman who's trying to take over the world, we're also trapped in your homework.'

'Stop arguing, you two,' Mum said. 'You heard Pratt. This may be an illusion but it won't feel like one. We may not be able to physically hurt ourselves but we can certainly feel pain. We need to be careful.'

Emma punched me in the arm.

'Ouch!' I said.

Emma nodded.

'You're right, Mum. We can feel pain.' She punched me again. 'But since this is all his fault, why don't we just knock him out? Maybe if Mark's unconscious, Pratt won't be able to control his mind.'

I had the feeling Emma just wanted to hit me a lot.

'I'm afraid Pratt is using Mark's *subconscious* mind,' Mum replied. 'Even if he was asleep, Mark couldn't control this.'

Emma tutted. 'Great,' she said. 'Disaster Boy isn't much use when he's awake either.'

There was a loud crack and a bolt of lightning forked across the sky. Mum looked up and frowned. The lightning looked like the energy that had shot from the grey disc inside Pratt's machine.

'All right everyone,' Dad said. 'I have this under control. Stand back.'

He strode forward and held up his hand. The men in animal skins murmured, muttered and raised their weapons. I had no idea how many there were, they seemed to be everywhere. They surrounded the stones. Behind them, I saw small fires burning and other groups huddled together. I had the feeling we'd interrupted some kind of meeting.

'Hello!' Dad shouted. 'It's good to see you all. Now, I know it must seem a bit strange, us appearing out of nowhere, but I promise you, there's nothing to worry about. Just stay calm and everything will be fine.'

'Robert,' Mum said. 'I know we're in England but this is probably the fourteenth century BC, not the twenty-first century AD. They don't understand what you're saying.'

'Right,' Dad replied. 'I hadn't thought of that. Let me try something else.' He took another step forward. 'Hel-lo,' he said a bit more loudly and a bit more slowly. 'Now, there's no need to worry. We won't hurt you. Just . . . stay . . . calm!'

Dad had done it again, he'd told a group of people there was nothing to worry about, and even though they didn't understand him, it had the same effect. To be fair, it probably wasn't Dad's fault that the men in animal skins yelled, roared and ran

away. It probably had something to do with the figure who soared over our heads. He swooped up and down, did a loop the loop and left a sparkling gold trail behind him.

After whizzing over Stonehenge, he circled back and landed between us and the stones.

'Who's that?' Emma asked, punching me again. 'And what's he doing in *your* mind?'

If I'd been in control of my power even a little, I would have made a big hole appear in front of me and jumped into it. I couldn't believe what I was seeing. It was me ... or rather, it was the superhero I imagined I wanted to be when I was old enough to stop being called Dynamic *Boy*. He was a daydream, the kind of silly, cartoon super-man who was strong enough to lift mountains and could fly faster than a speeding bullet. To be honest, he wouldn't even have looked good in a comic. And yet there he was, standing in front of me, legs apart, hands on his hips, chest stuck out with my face on his head!

'So Captain Valiant,' he bellowed,

'you would dare to challenge Wotan the Mighty? Well, this time you have met your match! Ha, ha, ha! Wotan fears no man, not even the great Captain Valiant. There is no one mightier than Wotan!'

He even had a stupid name like me! Wotan the Mighty hadn't sounded so bad in my imagination. Now it sounded terrible. And his catchphrase, *There is no one mightier than Wotan* . . . It had worked in my head. Now it just seemed silly.

'Wotan the what?' Emma smirked.

Dad looked at me. 'Are you responsible for that?' he asked.

'Well . . .' I replied, 'sort of . . . I suppose.'

Mum put her arm round my shoulder. 'Don't worry about it, Mark,' she said. 'I'm sure if Pratt got into our minds he would find things which are just as . . .' She glanced at Wotan and choked back a laugh. '. . . curious.'

Mum was being kind. Wotan was more than curious. He was ridiculous. In my dreams, he was never really a complete person. He was an idea.

He did the things I couldn't do. Now that he was sort of real, it was obvious I hadn't thought the idea through properly.

Wotan was unnaturally tall with thick, muscular arms and legs. His chest and stomach looked like carved stone. His head was almost square. His black hair shone as if it had been painted and his blue eyes glittered like glass. His mouth was fixed in a smile, which showed an impossible number of teeth. They gleamed and sparkled like the lights on a Christmas tree.

If that had been the worst of it, I could have coped. You see, I'd always struggled to think of a costume for Wotan. Sometimes it was black, sometimes it was red, sometimes there were silver stripes, sometimes the stripes were gold. But of all the things I imagined, I never dressed Wotan in only a pair of red and black boxer shorts with silver lightning bolts down the front.

If this is what Pratt had found in my imagination, I needed therapy!

'Well, Captain Valiant, are you up to the

challenge?' Wotan said, throwing his head back and laughing. 'Ha, ha, ha! No one can match the power of Wotan the Mighty! I am invincible!'

'I wish you were invisible,' I muttered.

Wotan bounded away. He cleared the distance between himself and Stonehenge in two strides. Then, with another laugh, he picked up one of the standing stones and threw it at us. The rock rose in

a graceful, elegant arc. It seemed to hang in mid-air for a moment, then began its descent. We were all so amazed at the sight we almost forgot to move.

Mum was the first to come to her senses. She pulled me and Emma out of the way as the rock's shadow fell across us. The stone thudded into the ground, upright and balanced on its end. Dad wasn't so quick to get out of the way. Although the boom of the rock's landing made him jump, he merely stared at the stone and watched it teeter. He only realised what was happening as the slab fell towards him. His fist swung up and smashed it to pieces.

'Dad, look out!' I cried.

My warning came too late. Wotan had already attacked again. The half-dressed superhero flew across the grass like an arrow. Dad only had time to turn round before Wotan's fist hit him in the stomach.

The next thing we knew, Wotan stood in front of us with his hands on his hips, laughing and flashing his teeth. Dad had gone. He'd shot off, cutting a deep, muddy groove in the ground as his body tumbled over and over.

'Ha, ha, ha!' Wotan said. 'There is no one mightier than Wotan! He is the mightiest of them all! Ha, ha, ha!' He flexed his muscles. 'Fear not, for Wotan is a friend to the weak and helpless.

No woman or child need dread the power of Wotan!'

'But you nearly hit us with that stone,' Emma said.

Wotan threw his head back and laughed again. 'Ha, ha, ha! There is no one mightier than Wotan!'

'Oh really?' Emma glared at him. 'We'll see about that!'

Wotan was still laughing when Emma used her

power to move objects with her mind, turned him upside down and threw him back across the grass into Stonehenge. He even laughed as he bounced between the stones. The grey slabs cracked and crunched as he hit them.

His laughter only made Emma more determined to hurt him. She clenched her fists, gritted her teeth and made a strange growling noise.

Wotan landed on his back in the middle of the stones. 'Ha ha, ha! No one is mightier than Wotan!' he said, trying to stand – only Emma didn't give him a chance to get up.

One by one, she lifted the standing stones and slammed them down on Wotan. Slab by slab, Emma pulled apart the stone circle and rebuilt it on top of him. He disappeared under a pile of huge grey rocks.

By the time Emma had finished, Stonehenge had been turned into a lopsided pyramid. It looked quite good.

I thought it made a far more interesting tourist attraction than the original Stonehenge.

'There, that should keep him quiet,' Emma said.

It didn't. No sooner had the last of the slabs settled on the top of the pyramid than we heard, 'Ha, ha, ha! There is no one mightier than Wotan!' and he shot out of the stones, blowing the pyramid apart.

To make matters worse, he was now naked. His boxer shorts must have got caught in the stones. He landed between us and Stonehenge. He stood with his hands on his hips, stuck out his chest, flashed his teeth and laughed.

'Ha, ha, ha! Wotan is the mightiest of them all! No one can match the power of Wotan!'

'Will you please shut up?!' Dad shouted.

Emma must have given him the idea. Dad flew over Wotan holding a huge grey slab. He raised the slab over his head and smashed Wotan into the ground. Again and again, Dad brought the stone crashing down. It boomed like a drum. The stone became a grey blur. Soon, it had broken in two, then in three, then in four, but that didn't stop Dad. It wasn't until the stone was in bits and he had to stamp on a pile of rubble that Dad finally gave up.

'Who's the mightiest now?!' he said, kicking the rubble.

There was a roar behind him. Dad turned and saw the men in animal skins rushing towards him. At the same time, a hand shot out of the rubble and grabbed his ankle. Wotan's head popped up between Dad's feet.

'Ha, ha, ha! No one is mightier than Wotan!'

Dad tried to fly away but Wotan held him tight. The men were getting closer. Spears whistled through the air and clattered on the stone. Dad was in trouble. He couldn't fight Wotan and the men at the same time. Even though this was only an illusion, there was no telling what might happen. We had to do something . . . or *I* had to do something. After all, this was my power we were fighting.

'Hold on, Dad!' I shouted. 'Leave this to me!'

I only planned to create a small illusion,

something which would frighten the men in animal skins. It wasn't going to be anything spectacular, maybe a dinosaur or something. And not even a dangerous dinosaur like tyrannosaurus rex. I was thinking something like triceratops or brontosaurus.

But I didn't get the chance. No sooner had I started to use my powers than there was a crack and lightning flashed across the sky. Just like before, the lightning reminded me of the energy that had shot down the walls of Pratt's machine.

It snaked from horizon to horizon like a net and then flowed across the ground in glittering strands.

Thankfully, Mum reacted quicker than me. Sometimes, it's really useful having a mum who's super-fast. I was out of the way before I realised what was happening. The energy seemed to be heading for me. I stopped trying to create an illusion as it hit the spot where I'd been standing.

There was an explosion of light. The energy crackled and sparked in a twisting column.

'Get back!' Mum shouted. 'Whatever you do, don't touch it!'

Mum needn't have worried. I hadn't planned to go anywhere near it. Although I did wonder, when the ground started to shake, the grass started to bulge and the first building exploded out of the ground, whether the lightning was the least of our problems.

CHAPTER 7

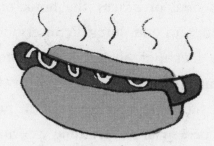

'You know what?' Emma said, picking stones out of her hair. 'You really have a weird imagination.'

I thought Emma was being a bit unfair. As I lifted my head and blinked to clear my vision, I was quite happy with what I saw. After Stonehenge and Wotan, the place we now found ourselves in was almost normal . . . almost. All right, so maybe it had risen out of the ground, and maybe instead of a stone circle and grass we were now surrounded by skyscrapers, and maybe Wotan and the men in animals skins had been replaced by ordinary people in ordinary clothes, but at least it all looked normal.

We were back in the modern world. There were cars, buses and lorries. Traffic signals flashed. I heard the squeal of brakes, the honk of horns, hurrying footsteps and garbled conversations. If I ignored the fact that all this had erupted from under us and that we were covered in dirt and stones while sitting on a pavement in the middle of a stream of pedestrians, everything was fine.

After all, I don't suppose it really mattered that

we were outside a metal gate which had *Welcome to Flushing Meadows* written on it. And I don't suppose it mattered that we had gone from fourteenth-century BC England to twenty-first century AD New York. The most important thing was that we were all right. The lightning had gone, the earthquake had passed and none of us were hurt.

Given the things that Pratt could have found in my mind, this was fine. There couldn't be much to hurt us here.

'Flushing Meadows,' Dad said, pointing at the metal gate. 'That was the place on television this morning. You know, where that mobile phone took pictures of people going to the toilet.'

Mum got up, shook dust and dirt off her costume, and studied the sign. She ran her fingers over the gate. She then looked round at the people who walked past us. No one seemed to notice we were there.

That's when I realised I was fooling myself if I thought anything about this place was normal. Superheroes don't get ignored when they stand in the middle of a busy street. People either get very nervous or very excited when we're around. If they don't want our autograph or a picture, then they're usually running away from something mean and nasty that we've come to fight.

The meanest and nastiest thing on the street was Emma, and no one was bothered about her.

'Look over there,' Mum said. 'On the other side of the gate, it's the Lunch Monkey Café.'

She pushed the gate open. The hinges

squeaked. She closed the gate, pushed it open again and listened to the squeak. She nodded to herself as if the squeak was important.

'Another illusion,' she said, 'and another world which seems real. But why did it all change?' She looked at me. 'Mark, were you trying to use your power before the lightning struck?'

'Yes,' I replied. 'I was trying to help Dad.'

Mum opened and closed the gate again. The squeak was louder this time; or maybe it only sounded louder because I listened to the gate the way Mum did.

'So you tried to use your power, the lightning struck and the illusion changed.' Mum looked up into the sky. 'Do you remember Pratt said something about feedback in the neural net? It hurt him. And do you remember just now, when

the lightning struck, it headed for you, Mark? I pulled you out of the way because I thought . . . It must be the feedback. The lightning is some kind of feedback. Pratt's machine is working too hard. The neural net is unstable. That's why he wants to build a more powerful version. He said this one is only a prototype. It was never designed to —'

'If you want my opinion,' Emma said, charging through the gate and heading for the café, 'the biggest mistake Pratt made was trying to control the mind of Boring Boy. Do you know, it's so embarrassing having a brother who doesn't have at least one sun-drenched beach in his head. If Pratt was using my mind we'd be in Bali by now. Instead, we get standing stones and skyscrapers!' She glared at me. 'You may not be in control of these illusions, Dreary Boy, but if I can't get something decent to eat in this place, I'm going to create a website for that thing – Wotan the Mighty – and make sure everyone knows you're his number one fan!'

Emma walked through the door and slammed it shut.

Dad nudged me. 'Are you sure she's not an illusion?' he asked.

I shook my head. 'Even I couldn't create something that horrible,' I replied.

We followed Emma inside the café. Dad and I were happy to go in after her. Mum wasn't as keen. She didn't say anything, but I knew she had more important things to think about than what was on the menu of the Lunch Monkey Café. While we were stuck here, Pratt was working on his plan to build a criminal empire. We should have been doing something a bit more heroic than ordering coffee and muffins! When the four of us sat at a table by the window, Mum frowned and shook her head as if she was angry with herself. 'What can I get you?' the waitress asked. She was a young, dark-haired

woman who looked as if she had something better to do than take our order. I don't know what; we were the only customers in the café.

'Bring me the biggest burger on the menu,' Emma said. 'And your largest ice cream.' She folded her arms and smiled. 'If this is an illusion, that means there are no calories and no fat. I can eat what I like.'

The waitress didn't move. She tapped her pencil on her pad and yawned.

'Is that the same for all of you?' she asked.

I went to reply but couldn't get the words out. I don't know why I hadn't realised it before, but the waitress . . . I recognised her. And if the grin now on Emma's face was anything to go by, so had she.

'Excuse me,'
Emma said to
the waitress,
'I don't mean
to be rude,
but is your
name Amy?'

The waitress shrugged. 'What if it is?'

'No reason,' Emma said. 'I just wondered if you had a younger brother named Darren who used to play football for his school?'

I suddenly felt very hot. Darren had been in my class last year. He'd moved when his father got a new job. His sister had been in Year 11. She was one of those girls it was impossible for a boy to ignore.

'Look, do you want something to eat or not?' the waitress asked.

Dad took control of the situation. 'Can we see the menu?' he said.

A grubby, dog-eared square of card landed on the table.

'I'll give you a few minutes,' the waitress said and walked away.

When she had gone, Emma leered at me. 'That's Amy Jenkins,' she said. 'You have Amy Jenkins in your imagination. She's one of my friends on Facebook. Wait until we get home. I'm going to post a message on her wall. You fancy her!'

'Stop it, Emma,' Mum said. 'Leave Mark alone.

Don't blame him for what's in his subconscious mind. Our thoughts are meant to be private. I'm sure you wouldn't like it if Pratt was going through your head.'

Emma sniggered, sat back and mouthed at me, 'You fancy Amy Jenkins.'

Dad picked up the menu and read it. He nodded in approval. 'Now this is my kind of food,' he said. 'Bacon and egg; sausage and egg; bacon, egg and chips;

sausage, egg and chips; bacon, egg, chips and beans; sausage, egg, chips and beans; bacon, sausage, egg, chips, beans and spam; sausage, egg, chips, beans and spam; bacon, egg, spam, chips, beans and spam; sausage, egg, spam, chips, beans and spam.' He paused. 'There's a lot of spam on this menu.'

Emma kicked me under the table. 'You fancy Amy Jenkins,' she whispered.

Mum snatched the menu from Dad. She looked at it in disgust. 'So is this in your imagination as well?' she said, holding the menu in front of me. 'After everything I've told you about eating healthy food and after all the effort I put into cooking your meals, this is the thanks I get? You secretly dream of bacon, egg, sausage, chips and beans. Is that what you really want?'

'Don't forget the spam,' Dad said.

'Shut up, Robert!'

I groaned and slumped forward. My head banged on the table.

'None of this is real,' I said. 'It's in my imagination. Don't you think I would have stopped this from happening if I could control my imagination?'

'You fancy Amy Jenkins,' Emma whispered again.

That was it. I'd had enough. I'd show her what it was like to have someone going through your mind. I'd make her look stupid and see if she liked it. Emma hated spiders. Well, how would she feel if there was one crawling up her leg or down her face?

That would stop her going on about Amy Jenkins! I thought about it. I wanted it to happen, and I was going to make it happen – but then I remembered. The last time I'd tried to create an illusion the lightning had struck and the world around us had changed. At the moment, I was quite happy with this world. After all, if I had to be stuck in an illusion, I'd rather be in an illusion with Amy Jenkins than Wotan the Mighty.

'Look,' the waitress said, coming up to our table again and slapping her pad down, 'are you ready to order? I've a lot to do.'

Mum stood up. 'So do we,' she said, pushing us out of our seats and herding us towards the door.

'We're not hungry.'

'I am,' Dad said.

As soon as we were outside, Mum faced us. 'I think I've worked out a way of escaping from these illusions!' she said, pointing at the sky. 'It's the lightning, or rather it's the feedback. Pratt's machine is working too hard. It's overloaded, and I think I know what we can do about it. We have to use the lightning to force the machine to shut down . . .' She gave me one of her serious looks. ' . . . or blow up. Either way, we don't have a choice. We have to stop Pratt.'

I didn't like the sound of that. How could we control the lightning? I couldn't even control the illusions. And as for blowing the machine up, that sounded really bad – we were inside it!

No one else seemed bothered though.

Emma muttered something about Amy Jenkins again and all Dad did was look back at the café and ask, 'Can't we have a takeaway?'

CHAPTER 8

I suppose I would have been more confident in what Mum said if she'd sounded a bit more certain that her idea would work. I understood why she wasn't. She may have been super-clever but even she didn't know how Pratt's machine operated. She hadn't designed or built it. Maybe the lightning wasn't feedback and was part of the machine's ordinary working. Or maybe Mum *was* right and the machine did have a problem.

Whatever we did, it was going to be risky.

The gate squeaked as Mum went back into the street and we followed her. Once again, we were in the middle of streams of people crowding past on either side. Many wore business suits and carried briefcases and mobile phones. They were all talking even though no one was listening to what anyone said. Every face I saw had that

I-should-be-somewhere-else look. Hands waved at taxis and feet ran for buses.

The funny thing was, despite all the waving and running, no one seemed to get anywhere. It looked as if everyone had somewhere to go, only they all got in each other's way and ended up going nowhere. Of course, we only made matters worse by standing in the middle of the pavement. But that didn't matter. They weren't real people and this wasn't a real street. The buildings around us were imaginary, so were the cars, buses and lorries. Even the smell of exhaust fumes was an illusion – at least, that's what I kept telling myself.

'It's definitely the lightning,' Mum said again. 'I knew there was something wrong when Pratt got that shock in his chair. He must be trying to do something the machine wasn't designed to do. He's transferring Mark's thoughts into our minds, but the machine was only designed to transmit his thoughts into one person's mind.'

She tapped her head.

'That's why he put the processor in his brain.

He's part of the neural net. Only now, the net has to deal with five minds rather than two, that's why it's overloaded.' She glanced at me. 'And that's why, when Mark tried to use his powers at the same time as Pratt, the system couldn't cope. It had to reset. That's what happened at Stonehenge. But we need to shut it down. How can we create an energy surge powerful enough to shut the system down?'

Dad's stomach growled. 'Sorry,' he said. 'I was thinking about bacon sandwiches.'

Emma chortled to herself. I knew she was going to say something else about Amy Jenkins. Thankfully, she didn't get the chance.

There was a scream. A woman came running through the crowd. I don't know if the others recognised her, but I did. She wore a light green top and a dark green skirt. Both were too tight. The last time I'd seen this woman, she'd also had a microphone in her hand.

It was the television reporter who'd been insulted by the cash machine. I remembered her because the cash machine had said green wasn't her colour. I also remembered what Emma had said, and she was right: the woman's bum was too big for her skirt.

The woman barged through the people, pushing and shoving everyone out of the way. Some distance behind her, also struggling through the crowd, was a television cameraman. He was finding it harder to get through because everyone tried to stop him. As soon as someone saw the camera on his shoulder, they blocked his way, got

out their mobile phone and tried to take a picture of themselves being filmed.

'You!' the woman shrieked, pointing at Dad. 'You in that silly costume! You're a superhero, aren't you?'

Dad was about reply when the woman grabbed him by the collar and pulled him close.

He tried to get free but she lifted him off the ground and shouted in his face.

'Don't say anything!' she yelled. 'I don't need you to speak. I need you to do something heroic. I need you to teach them a lesson!' She dropped Dad and pointed at the people around her. 'Look at them! They're all staring. Can't you see? Every morning they switch on their televisions and expect me to send them off to work with a smile. And what thanks do I get?' She pointed at her bottom. 'They say I have a big bum! But what's my bum got to do with anything? It's my face they should be looking at.' She grabbed Dad again. 'I want you to stop them looking at my bum!'

She spun round and glared at the crowd, hissing and growling like a cat. Dad spun round with her, his body as loose and limp as a doll. He made a strange gurgling noise. The woman threw him down and turned on the crowd. 'Stop looking at my bum!' she screamed at the gawping people.

Dad got to his feet. He was dizzy and took a few moments to focus on the woman. By the time he had, she looked as if she was about to grab him again. He backed away.

'Look,' Dad said, 'I'm sorry people keep looking at your . . . but this isn't the kind of thing superheroes deal with. We fight super villains and aliens. Now, if you're being threatened by a super villain or an alien, we can help. But I'm afraid we can't stop people looking at your bum.'

The woman poked Dad in the chest. 'Have you looked at my bum?' she asked.

Dad went red. He went as red as he had at breakfast when Mum said he had no problem watching a woman with a big bum.

'No,' he lied.

Emma nudged me. 'It's not her bum that's the problem,' she whispered. 'Have you seen the rest of her?'

I had. The woman was getting bigger. I had no idea why she was getting bigger, although I did remember seeing a film called *Attack Of The Fifty Foot Woman* advertised on a film channel recently. Maybe that had something to do with it.

'Are you telling me the truth?' the woman asked.

Dad went even redder. 'Yes,' he lied again.

'Then *why* aren't you looking at my bum?' she shrieked. 'What's wrong with it?'

Mum sighed. Emma groaned. Dad gulped.

The woman went red in the face, trembled and screamed so loudly it made her eyes bulge and her ears go purple. 'Men!' she bellowed. 'You're all the same!'

What happened next took everyone by surprise. Every hand held up a mobile phone and pointed it at the woman. The four of us tried to get away, but there were so many people, it was like trying to walk through a wall.

'You're all the same!' the woman screamed again. 'Every one of you! It's never about me, is it? It's always about my bum!'

And as she screamed, the woman got even bigger. It was as if she'd been inflated. Soon, she towered over the street with one foot on either side of the road. Cars crashed into each other trying to avoid her shoes as people ran through the arches of her heels.

'I'll show you,' the woman roared. 'If you want big, then you can have big!'

Like a bad-tempered child, the woman raised her feet and stamped on whatever was under them. The road buckled and the pavement cracked. People ran along the street, shouting and screaming. This only seemed to make the woman angrier. She kicked and punched the buildings. Windows shattered and walls crumbled. The woman picked up a bus and used it like a club, swinging it over her head and smashing it down on anything that moved.

'You know that idea you had,' I said to Mum.

'Well, maybe now is a good time to try it out.'

The bus flew over our heads. It smashed into the front of a department

store. It was quickly followed by a car, which the woman had kicked out of her way. As the people ran around her, the woman laughed and squashed them underfoot.

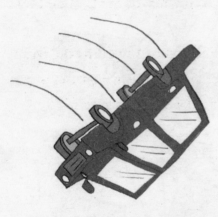

Mum glanced at me and nodded. She gripped Dad's arm and pointed along the street in the opposite direction to the woman.

'We need to be up there,' she said. 'Right at the top where the lightning rod is. You can carry me and Emma. Mark can fly by himself.'

I looked where Mum pointed. Emma must have done the same.

'Oh, that's just great,' Emma said. 'Now all we need is a giant gorilla and the day will be perfect!'

It was the Empire State Building. Mum wanted the four of us to get to the top of the Empire State Building!

'It's the best place for what I want to do,' Mum said. 'We need to create a massive power surge and I think I've worked out how to do it!'

CHAPTER 9

I was glad Mum had come up with a plan to get us out of these illusions because, at that exact moment, the world went dark and a fist hovered over our heads. I couldn't tell whether the woman with the fist was now fifty foot tall, but she was *very* big.

Dad was the first to react. He flew up and smashed into the fist. The woman yelled and pulled her hand back, like she'd been stung. She rubbed her fingers and glared at us. Then her foot came down. Dad raced for the heel but Emma got there first. She used her mind to twist the woman's ankle and tip her off balance. The woman fell back, crashing down on the street in a cloud of dust and glass.

'I hope you're sure about this, Louise,' Dad said, picking up Mum and Emma. 'I don't like the idea of being fried any more than I like the idea of being crushed.'

'Just get us to that lightning rod,' Mum said. 'You can moan at me later if this goes wrong!'

Behind us, coughing and spluttering, the woman pulled herself up. As we rose into the air, I heard her roar. A twisted car whizzed over our heads. Chunks of wall and pavement followed.

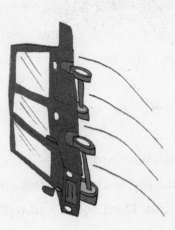

Thankfully, the woman's aim was terrible.

'Once we get to the top,' Mum shouted, 'we have to hold on to the rod. Then Mark will try to

create an illusion. If I'm right, his power will cause an overload in the machine's circuits and the lightning will strike. I'm hoping that the lightning rod will act as a reality conduit and overload the neural net. That should shut the machine down.'

'Although I didn't understand a word of that,' Emma said, 'it sounds like something that's going to hurt.'

'It will,' Mum replied. 'Because if it doesn't hurt, it won't work!'

The woman's aim was now so bad that she missed with everything she threw. As we flew over the streets, all sorts of vehicles bounced off the buildings before falling to the ground. By the time we reached the top of the Empire State Building, although the woman still raged, she was a long way behind.

Dad put Mum and Emma down and the two of them grasped the metal pole. Dad and I hovered close to the rod, ready to take hold when we needed to. Mum looked up into the sky. For a moment, as I followed her gaze and looked across the city, I found myself admiring the view.

It was easy to forget none of this was real. I may not have thought much of my powers of illusion, but when I saw what Pratt had done with them, I was impressed.

'Mark, it's time,' Mum said. She looked at Dad and Emma. 'Everybody hold on. Whatever happens, don't let go of the rod.' She shrugged. 'I'll be honest with you. I'm not sure if this will work.'

'And what happens if it doesn't?' Emma asked.

'Then Pratt will have won,' Mum replied. 'If we can't escape and he gets away, he'll do what he said and build another machine more powerful than this one. Then he really will take over the world.'

'No pressure then,' Emma muttered. She closed her eyes and tightened her grip on the rod. 'I bet this messes up my hair.'

I wasn't really sure what sort of illusion Mum wanted me to create. I thought something harmless would be best – like clouds, birds and a hot air balloon. As I imagined those things, there was a crack and a bolt of energy shot across the sky. The glittering strands of the neural net started to snake from horizon to horizon.

'That's it, Mark,' Mum said. 'The system is starting to overload. Keep going.'

And I would have kept going, if not for the fact that the building shook and Mum lost her balance. She toppled backwards and fell. Dad was quick enough to dive down and grab her, but he wasn't quick enough to get clear of the hand that shot up and caught him and Mum in mid-air.

It was the fifty-foot woman. She was climbing up the side of Empire State Building. She had smashed her fist and feet into the bricks to create handholds and footholds and was now pulling herself up towards us!

'Mark!' Mum shouted from between the woman's fingers. 'Don't lose your concentration. Create an illusion now!'

'But what about you?' I cried. Emma reached up and grabbed my arm.

'No one else can do this, Mark,' she said. 'We need you to use your power. You have to get us out of here!'

The strands of the neural net were coming closer, twisting through the streets and over the buildings. I had to trust Mum was right. I had to create an illusion. But then the whole building started to tilt. The weight of the fifty-foot woman was pulling it over. The lightning rod bent and snapped at the base. There was no more time. I had to make the lightning strike!

The illusion took shape. I saw it all: the clouds, the birds and the balloon. I saw the colours, I heard the sounds and, in that moment, the sky went white. There was an echoing

and my whole body shook.

Mum had said it would hurt and she wasn't wrong. It was as if I had fallen into a wasps' nest. My skin felt like it was being stabbed by thousands of needles over and over again. I closed my eyes and yelled. I lost my grip and fell.

But I wasn't bothered about the fall. I was bothered about the pain. It pulled me down, dragging me further and further into its grip, and the more I cried out, the more it hurt. There seemed to be no escape. There seemed to be no way to make it stop.

And then, as quickly as it came, the pain was gone. It just stopped. Rather than feeling as if I was being pricked by needles, my skin felt cool and tingly. I opened my eyes and found myself lying on the floor of Pratt's secret base. Above me, I saw the black and white tiles that lined the ceiling. Around me, I heard groans and gasps.

We were back. Mum's plan had worked.

'Is everyone OK?' Dad struggled to his feet. He went across to Mum and helped her up. 'Emma? Mark? Are you all right?'

'I think so,' I replied.

'I'm not,' Emma said. 'My hair's gone all frizzy!'

'Count yourself lucky,' another voice said. 'At least you have hair.'

It was Pratt. He lay on the floor near his chair. If he hadn't spoken, I would have thought he was dead. He had been burnt very badly. His clothes were smouldering rags. The skin on his arms and legs looked like it had melted. Smoke snaked out of the hole in his head.

'Well, at least my plan almost worked,' he

coughed, holding up a charred hand and looking at the blackened fingers. 'Maybe next time I won't plug myself into the machine.'

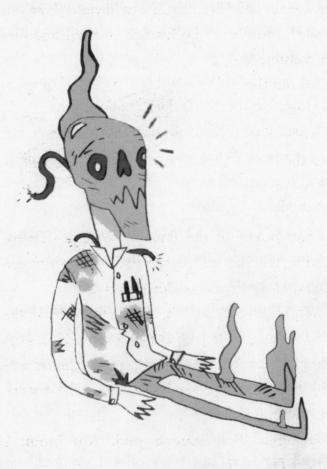

He tried to raise himself but couldn't. His arms and legs wouldn't work. He collapsed to the floor. We gathered round him, even though there wasn't much we could do to help. It was obvious Pratt was finished. Mum knelt by his side. She reached into her costume and pulled out the flash drive I had seen her take from the lab before we left home.

Pratt looked at the flash drive and grunted. Then he reached up to grab me, only he was too weak and his fingers couldn't hold on.

'Who'd have thought it, eh? Algernon Pratt, the Silver Cyborg, beaten by Dynamo Boy.' Pratt's lips twisted in what might have been a grin. It was hard to tell. His face, like his machine, didn't work properly any more.

'Dynamic Boy,' Emma said. 'My brother's name is Dynamic Boy.'

Pratt laughed and groaned at the same time. 'Who cares what he's called. He still beat me.' He winced. 'Next time, I'll have to deal with him first.'

Mum held up the flash drive. 'There won't be a next time, Algernon,' she said. 'On this drive is a variation of the virus you used to attack my system. In a few minutes, if I can find a working port, I'm going to upload it and destroy all your files. A machine like this is too dangerous. When the government get here and pick over what's left of you and your machine, they're going to find nothing but burnt-out circuits and a burnt-out man.'

Pratt tried to laugh again. He could only gasp for air. 'Of course they are, Ms Victory,' he said.

'And do you think I care what those idiots find? You should know by now that I'm not the sort of person who wouldn't have a back-up plan. I'm the Silver Cyborg. I'm the world's greatest computer genius. With a machine like this, I can put my ideas into the minds of men and women in very important positions. And that's exactly what I've done. They're out in the world, Ms Victory, thinking my thoughts and developing my plans. I may have lost this battle but trust me, the war between us isn't over.'

He pointed a burnt finger at me. 'Remember what I said, Dynamic Boy. The next time we meet, I'll deal with you first.'

Pratt coughed. Sparks shot from the hole in his head and he slumped back, his metal skull clanging against the floor.

'I think he's blown a fuse,' Emma said.

'He's done more than that,' Mum said. She looked at the flash drive in her hand. 'It's time to get to work. Robert, start pulling the panels off the wall. There has to be some kind of port or input somewhere. We need to find it quickly. We need to make sure this system is offline for good.'

Dad did as he was told. Black and white panels clanged to the floor as Mum went searching for a way to upload the virus. While the two of them worked, Emma stood next to me.

'Pratt was right, you know,' she said as we watched Dad tear the building apart. '*You* were the one who beat him. If it wasn't for your power, we wouldn't have escaped.'

'If it wasn't for my power, we wouldn't have been trapped in the first place,' I replied.

Emma thought for a few moments. 'True,' she said, 'but that doesn't change the fact that you're the one who saved us. Your powers really are quite impressive, you know. Don't let anyone tell you they're not. I'll have a lot more respect for them, and you, after this.'

I couldn't believe what I heard. 'Do you mean that?' I asked.

Emma sniggered. 'Of course I don't,' she replied. 'Let's be honest, that's one illusion neither of us would ever believe.'

CAPTAIN VALIANT

And me

REVENGE OF THE BLACK PHANTOM

Mark Taylor seems to be an average schoolboy,
but he's really Dynamic Boy!
He and his family – Captain Valiant, Ms Victory
and Moon Girl – are a superhero team. If only his
name, costume and superpower weren't so
rubbish, Dynamic Boy might enjoy saving the
world from baddies . . .
But when people start turning into monsters,
they all realise this is no ordinary baddy –
it's the revenge of the Black Phantom.

CAPTAIN VALIANT

And me

THE MAN WHO STOLE A PLANET

While attempting to stop a spaceship crashing into Earth, Dynamic Boy and his superhero family get caught up in a battle between the Federal Army of the Republic of Taranos (FART) and the Bureau of Undercover Research Personnel (BURP).

An agent of the BURP has stolen a secret weapon belonging to the FART – the Eternity Stone, a device which can shrink planets to the size of a matchbox.

But can the Eternity Stone be recaptured before the galaxy falls to FART domination?

piccadillypress.co.uk/children

Go online to discover:

☆ more books you'll love

☆ competitions

 sneak peeks inside books

☆ fun activities and downloads